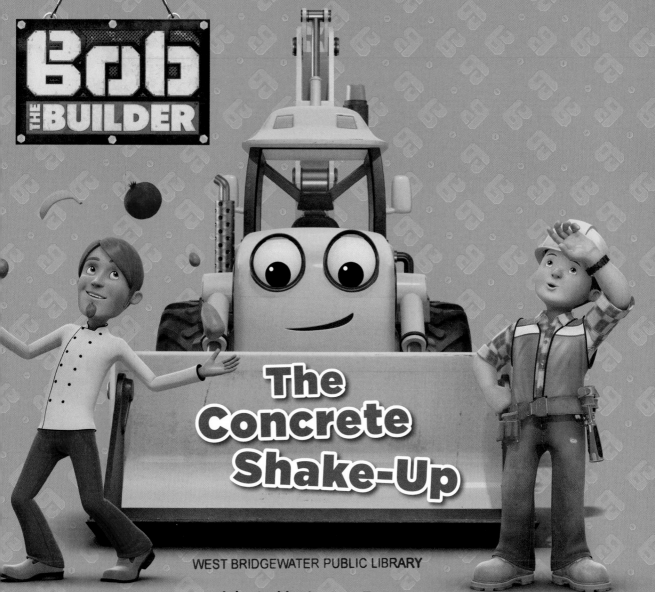

Bob the Builder

The Concrete Shake-Up

Adapted by Lauren Forte
Based on the screenplay by Laura Beaumont & Paul Larson

LITTLE, BROWN & COMPANY
LB kids

Little, Brown and Company

Hachette Book Group
1290 Avenue of the Americas, New York, NY 10104
Visit us at lb-kids.com
bobthebuilder.com

LB kids is an imprint of Little, Brown and Company.
The LB kids name and logo are trademarks of Hachette Book Group, Inc.

The publisher is not responsible for websites (or their content) that are not owned by the publisher.

First Edition: July 2016

Library of Congress Control Number: 2016930418

ISBN 978-0-316-35584-1

10 9 8 7 6 5 4 3 2 1

CW

Printed in the United States of America

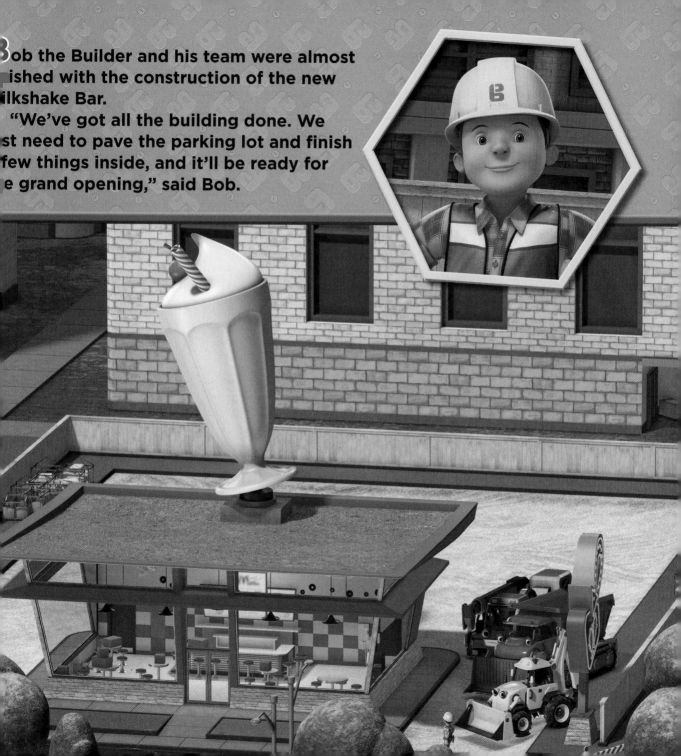

Bob the Builder and his team were almost finished with the construction of the new Milkshake Bar.

"We've got all the building done. We just need to pave the parking lot and finish a few things inside, and it'll be ready for the grand opening," said Bob.

"It's spectacular!" cheered Lofty.

Scoop agreed. "Especially that giant milkshake!"

"Wait until Wendy gets to work on it," Bob told them. "Once she puts the motor in and hooks up the electricity, it will spin around."

"Spin around?" cried Muck. "But that will spill the milkshake!"
"It's not a *real* milkshake, Muck!" Lofty laughed.
"I knew that," Muck answered shyly.

Suddenly, Chef Tattie walked up.
"What are you doing here, Chef?" asked Bob. "We're not finished yet!"
"I couldn't wait to get started!" Chef Tattie replied. "While you finish the Milkshake Bar and parking lot, I'll create the Tattielicious Shaketastic Surprise!"

"Brilliant!" Scoop shouted. "What's in it?"

"I've got no idea!" Chef Tattie admitted. "I love experimenting with new ingredients! I mix them up and see what comes out!"

"Wow," Scoop replied.

"Okay, team!" cheered Bob. "Let's get started by mixing the concrete for the parking lot! SO...CAN WE BUILD IT?"

"YES, WE CAN!"

the team shouted back.

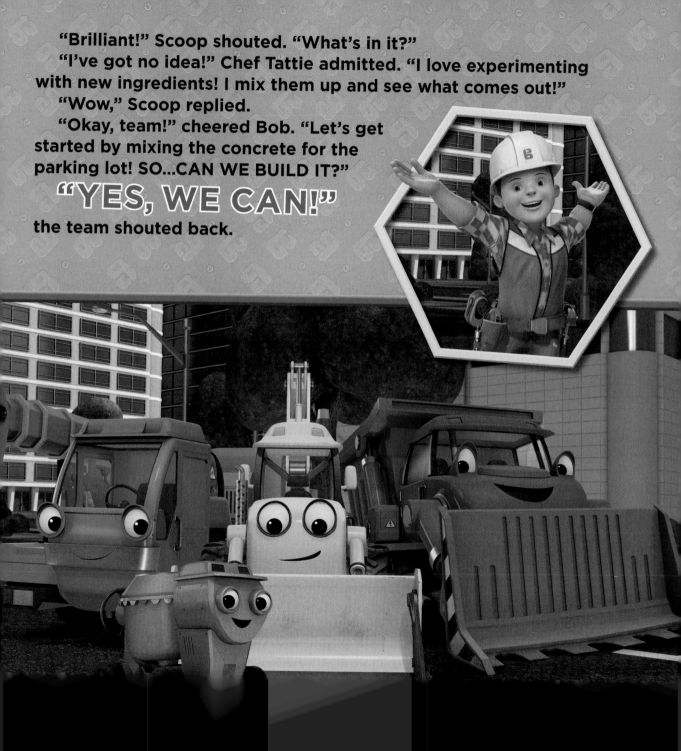

Scoop and Two-Tonne began gathering the supplies to mix the concrete.

"Hey, Two-Tonne!" Scoop called. "Chef Tattie's Milkshake Bar is going to be really fun. So, what if we did something *more* fun with the concrete?"

"More fun?" asked Two-Tonne.

"Maybe we can be like Chef Tattie," Scoop explained. "Experiment with some new ingredients...mix something up...and see what comes out."

"Oh no," replied Two-Tonne. "I never mess with concrete. We'll be making the usual concrete. Flat, smooth, and very, very gray."

"Oh..." Scoop sighed. He was disappointed. He wanted to experiment!

Meanwhile, Bob and Wendy were adding the final touches inside the Milkshake Bar. Once everything was in place, they sat down in front of Chef Tattie.

"Let's try a bit of this! And one of those...a couple of these..." Chef Tattie said. "I *love* trying new mixtures and creating new colors!"

He was juggling fruit, bouncing berries, and even tossing ice cream and milk into the blender.

"I need someone to test out my creations and tell me which one is truly the most shaketastic!" he cried.

"I'll do it!" Wendy quickly volunteered.

Chef Tattie made many different milkshakes,
and Wendy tried each one!
"They are all great!" Wendy declared.

Scoop watched Wendy sample the different milkshakes. He looked sad.

"What's wrong, Scoop?" Muck asked.

"I wanted to make fun concrete for Chef Tattie's Milkshake Bar parking lot, but Two-Tonne just wants to make the usual, boring concrete."

As Muck and Scoop watched Chef Tattie throw ingredients into his blender, they slowly smiled at each other. They had the same idea.

"There's no way I am going to make the usual concrete!"
Scoop announced. "I will be mixing up a Scoopilicious
Concretetastic Surprise!"

Muck was suddenly feeling unsure. "Err...are you sure
Two-Tonne will be okay with that?"

"He doesn't have to know!" Scoop said as he filled his
bucket with wood chips. Then he went to the trash bin and
took some things from there.

"Now, Scoop, measure out the ingredients correctly, or it just won't work!" stated Two-Tonne.

"Got it!" Scoop yelled. Then he dropped his special materials into Two-Tonne's hopper with the rest of the concrete.

"*Ahhh*...there's nothing like the usual concrete..." Two-Tonne said as he mixed and poured the concrete.

"This will be nothing like the usual concrete," Scoop said softly.

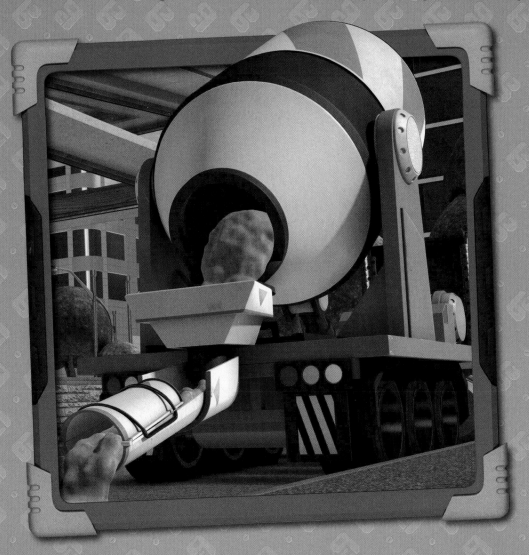

When they were done, Bob sent them home for the night. Scoop fell right to sleep, but Muck was restless.

"*Pssst!* Scoop? *Scooop?* SCOOP! Are you asleep?" Muck asked.

"Well, not now," Scoop answered. "What's the matter?"

"I'm worried about your Scoopilicious Concretetastic whatever you called it," Muck said nervously.

"No need to worry, Muck!" Scoop said happily. "I guarantee that by the end of the day everyone will be talking about it!"

The next morning, Bob and the team arrived back at the site.
"Wow! The concrete looks amazing!" yelled Scoop as he drove
onto the parking lot. "It's *so* colorful and fun and"—Scoop's tires
began to sink into the sludgy concrete—"squishy and sticky..."
"This concrete's not dry!" cried Bob. "Scoop, get out of here!"

Lofty drove up beside the lot and stopped at the edge.
"This is the strangest concrete I've ever seen," he said
as he lifted a banana peel from the concrete.

"Well, you were right about one thing, Scoop,"
said Muck. "Everyone's talking about your concrete."

"Oh, Bob...this is all my fault!" moaned Scoop. "When I saw Chef Tattie experimenting with different colors and ingredients, it looked like so much fun that I wanted to try it, too."

Bob wasn't mad, but Scoop felt terrible. As Scoop drove back toward the parking lot, he said, "I'm really sorry, Bob. I'll go and clear it all off."

Bob felt sorry for Scoop as he watched him clear the messy concrete mixture. He could see how sad Scoop was.

"You know, I'd have never created my legendary Purple Fizzle-Crush Chunky Delight if I hadn't tried mixing red currants, rhubarb, and cheesy crackers," Chef Tattie said as he walked over to Bob.

"You just gave me an idea. Muck, take me back to the yard!" Bob exclaimed.

A short time later, Bob, Muck, and Dizzy arrived at the lot.

"Okay, Scoop!" Bob said. "I want you to try again using some fun ingredients that don't come out of the garbage!"

Muck lowered his bucket. It was loaded with supplies.

"Wow!" shouted Scoop. "Yellow, red, and blue cement! And crunchy gravel chunks, too!"

"It's quick-drying cement! I'll mix it all up for you!" cried Dizzy.

Dizzy mixed up the multicolored concrete and started to pour it on the newly cleared parking lot. Scoop helped lay it out, and Muck smoothed it down.

When it was all finished and dry, the team gathered to see how it looked.

"I love it!" Chef Tattie declared. "Now everyone can park in this awesome-looking lot *and* enjoy my Tattielicious Shaketastic Surprise! On to the grand opening!"

Bob and the team smiled happily. It was another job well done!